by Barbara Baker

ILLUSTRATED BY VERA ROSENBERRY

Dutton Children's Books • *New York*

For Anne Demerle
B.A.B.

Text copyright © 2003 by Barbara A. Baker
Illustrations copyright © 2003 by Vera Rosenberry
All rights reserved.

CIP Data is available.

Published in the United States 2003 by Dutton Children's Books,
a division of Penguin Putnam Books for Young Readers
345 Hudson Street, New York, New York 10014
www.penguinputnam.com
Printed in Hong Kong / China • First Edition
ISBN 0-525-47027-1
1   3   5   7   9   10   8   6   4   2

CONTENTS

YUMMY

Little Martin did not want

to eat his egg.

"Egg is good for you,"

said his mother.

"Let me see you

eat it *all* up."

"No," said Martin.

"Yucky."

"Egg is *yummy*,"

said his mother.

"And it will make you

big and strong."

Martin held out his spoon.

"You," he said.

"Yummy, yummy, yummy,"

said his mother.

She pretended to eat some egg.

"Now it is your turn, Martin."

Martin pretended
to eat some egg.
"Yummy, yummy,
yummy," he said.

"All done."
He pushed his
plate away.

"Martin," said his mother.
"How will you grow up
to be a big boy
if you don't eat your egg?"

"Banana," said Martin.

Martin's mother gave him

a banana.

"Yummy, yummy, yummy,"

said Martin.

And he ate it all up.

ALL READY

"Time to go to the park,"

said Martin's mother.

"Want my ball," said Martin.

"OK," said his mother.

So Martin got his big red ball.

He gave it to his mother to carry.

"All ready now?" she said.

"No," said Martin.

He got his pail

and his shovel.

He gave them

to his mother to carry.

"All ready now?" she said.

But Martin was not ready.

He wanted

his dandy-dumper dump truck,

his fast-flying skates,

and his super-speedy scooter.

"Martin, dear, Mommy can't carry

all of those things,"

said his mother.

So Martin got his wagon, too.

"Thank you, Martin,"

said his mother.

She put all the toys

into the wagon.

"All ready now?" she said.

Martin looked at the wagon.

It was full of toys.

Then he climbed

into the wagon, too.

"All ready now," said Martin.

"Pull me."

DON'T TOUCH

"Look, Martin,"

said his mother.

"All of your friends are

in the park today.

Isn't that nice?"

Carlos and Sam ran up to Martin.

They looked at his wagon.

It was full of toys.

"*Mine,*" said Martin.

"*Don't touch!*"

"Now, Martin,"
said his mother.
"Carlos and Sam are
your friends.
It's nice to share
with friends.
Isn't it?"

"No!" said Martin.

"Go away."

"Martin bad boy,"

said Carlos.

"Bad boy," said Sam.

"Martin is a *good* boy,"

said his mother.

"He will share in a little while.

Won't you, Martin?"

"*No,*" said Martin.

Carlos and Sam went away.

"Now, Martin,"

said his mother.

"What do you want

to play with?"

Martin looked at the wagon

full of toys.

He looked at his mother.

Then he ran to the swings.

"Push me," said Martin.

ALL WET

Martin ran over to the

water fountain.

"Pick me up," he said.

His mother picked him up.

She pressed the button.

Martin drank some cold water.

Then he stuck his finger

in the hole.

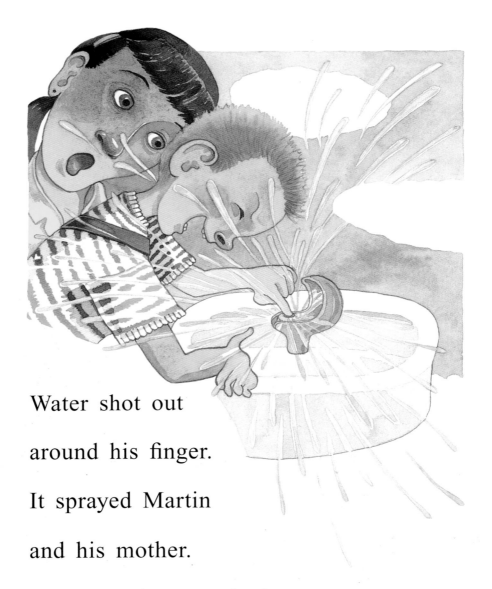

Water shot out
around his finger.
It sprayed Martin
and his mother.
"Now, Martin, you don't want
to get Mommy all wet. Do you?"

His mother put him down.

"More," yelled Martin.

"Pick me up."

"A little more,"

said his mother.

"But remember, this

water is for drinking."

She picked Martin up.

She pressed the button.

Martin stuck his finger

in the hole.

Martin's mother

got very wet.

"Time to go home,"

she said.

She took Martin over

to his wagon.

"NO!" cried Martin.

"No, no, NO!"

Carlos and Sam came over

to look.

Martin stopped crying.

"Me good boy," he said.

Then he gave his pail to Carlos.

He gave his shovel to Sam.

"How sweet," said Martin's mother.

"Martin is sharing his toys."

Martin took his dandy-dumper

dump truck.

Then Martin and Carlos

and Sam went to the sandbox.

Carlos looked at Martin.

"Dump truck?" he said.

He held out his hand.

"*Mine,*" said Martin.

"*Don't touch.*"

LITTLE ALICE

Martin was at home.

The doorbell rang.

Martin's mother went

to open the door.

"Oh, look, Martin," she said.

"Our new neighbors are here

for a visit."

Martin saw a lady

and a little girl.

"This is little Alice,"

said the lady.

"Hello," said Alice sweetly.

"And this is little Martin,"

said his mother.

"Say hello, Martin, dear."

"No," said Martin.

"Come inside, everyone,"

said Martin's mother.

"Alice, would you

like a cookie?"

Alice took a cookie.

"Thank you," she said.

Martin took one, too.

"What do you say, Martin?"

"*More*," said Martin.

Martin and Alice

went to play

in Martin's room.

"*My* toys," said Martin.

"Don't touch."

He made a monster face

at Alice.

Alice sat down on the floor.

She took something

out of her pocket.

"Lipstick," she said.

"Mommy's."

She put some on her mouth.

"Pretty."

Then she put some

on her nose.

"Me, too," said Martin.

Alice gave the lipstick to Martin.

Martin put some on his nose

and on his chin

and on his elbows.

"Now me," said Alice.

She put some on her chin

and her elbows

and her shoes.

Martin and Alice

put lipstick everywhere.

"Martin . . . Alice . . ."

called Martin's mother.

Martin and Alice

hid under the bed.

Martin's mother found them.

She was not happy.

She took them

to the living room.

"Oh, Alice!" said her mother.

She took Alice by the hand.

"Time to go home."

"Bye-bye," said Martin.

He gave Alice a little kiss.

"Oh, isn't that sweet,"

said Martin's mother.

Then she took Martin

to the sink.

She turned on the water.

"Me good boy," said Martin.

He smiled sweetly.

Then Martin stuck his finger

in the faucet.

48